P9-AOH-095

MOONGOBBLE AND ME
THE MISCHIEF MONSTER

Books by Bruce Coville

Rod Allbright and the Galactic Patrol
Aliens Ate My Homework
I Left My Sneakers in Dimension X
The Search for Snout
Aliens Stole My Body

Magic Shop Books
Jennifer Murdley's Toad
Jeremy Thatcher, Dragon Hatcher
The Monster's Ring

Moongobble and Me
The Dragon of Doom
The Weeping Werewolf
The Evil Elves

My Teacher Books
My Teacher Is an Alien
My Teacher Fried My Brains
My Teacher Glows in the Dark
My Teacher Flunked the Planet

The Dragonslayers

Goblins in the Castle

I Was a Sixth Grade Alien

AVAILABLE FROM SIMON & SCHUSTER

MOONGOBBLE AND ME

THE MISCHIEF MONSTER

Bruce Coville

ILLUSTRATED BY Katherine Coville

SIMON & SCHUSTER BOOKS FOR YOUNG READERS
New York London Toronto Sydney

For Bradley Dietz

SIMON & SCHUSTER BOOKS FOR YOUNG READERS
An imprint of Simon & Schuster Children's Publishing Division
1230 Avenue of the Americas, New York, NY 10020
Copyright © 2007 by Bruce Coville
Illustrations copyright © 2007 by Katherine Coville
All rights reserved, including the right of reproduction in whole or in part in any form.
SIMON & SCHUSTER BOOKS FOR YOUNG READERS
is a trademark of Simon & Schuster, Inc.
The text for this book is set in Historical Fell Type.
The illustrations for this book are rendered in graphite.
Manufactured in the United States of America
First S&S edition July 2007
2 4 6 8 10 9 7 5 3 1
Library of Congress Cataloging-in-Publication Data
Coville, Bruce.
The Mischief Monster / by Bruce Coville ; illustrated by Katherine Coville. — 1st S & S ed.
p. cm. —(Moongobble and me)
Summary: When the daughter of the Queen of the Mischief Monsters
runs away from home, it is up to Edward, Moongobble, Urk, and Fireball
to return her to Monster Mountain—then start a new quest.
ISBN-13: 978-1-4169-0807-4 (hardcover)
ISBN-10: 1-4169-0807-2 (hardcover)
[1. Fairy tales. 2. Magicians—Fiction. 3. Runaways—Fiction. 4. Monsters—Fiction.]
I. Coville, Katherine, ill. II. Title. III. Series: Coville, Bruce. Moongobble and me.
PZ8.C837Mis 2007
[Fic]—dc22
2006014769

CONTENTS

CHAPTER 1

STRANGE VISITOR

Sometimes when you get what you want, it's not as good as you thought it would be.

Here's what I mean. I was really happy when my friend Moongobble became a full magician. For one thing, it meant Fazwad would stop coming up with Mighty Tasks that Moongobble had to do if he wanted to join the Society of Magicians.

The problem was, life just wasn't as interesting without those Mighty Tasks. Oh, it was more interesting than it had been before Moongobble moved to Pigbone. But I had really liked going off

I

on the adventures—even if they did get kind of scary sometimes.

So I was feeling a little bored the morning Snelly came bursting into our lives.

I was staying with Moongobble for a few days while Mother and Father went to Flitwick City to sell some of Father's carvings. I was outside, working in the garden. Fireball, the little dragon who is my friend, had perched on a nearby tree branch. Whenever I got too hot, Fireball would flutter down to fan my face with his wings.

He had just flapped around my head a few times when he hissed, "What's that?"

"What's what?" I asked. Then I heard it too—a tiny voice, sobbing and wailing.

"It's coming from over there," I whispered.

Fireball settled onto my shoulder, hooking his tiny claws into my shirt. I put down my hoe, then dropped to my knees and began to crawl along the row of cabbages where I had been working.

The crying got louder.

"Waaaah! Waaaah! Oh, I am so miserable! Waaaah. . . ."

I pointed to a cabbage. Fireball nodded.

Moving as silently as possible, I lifted one of the big leaves. Beneath it sat a little person. She had her face buried in her hands and she was weeping as if her heart was broken. My own heart almost broke just listening to her!

"What's the matter?" I asked. "Why are you so unhappy?"

"Fooled ya!" cried the little creature. Then she jumped onto my head, mussed up my hair, scampered over my shoulders, and vanished among the cabbages.

I scrambled to my feet. She was nowhere in sight. Then I heard her laugh. It sounded like she was behind a tree. When I went to look, it turned out she had *climbed* the tree—which put her in a perfect position to pounce onto my shoulder.

"Got ya! Now you have to take me to see Moongobble."

"I would have taken you to him anyway, if you

had just asked," I said, trying to pull her loose.

This was true. It wasn't as if Moongobble had a lot of customers. And now that he was a full magician, he needed to find some. Otherwise he might have to go back to being a shoemaker.

When I finally managed to pry the creature off my shoulder, I held her in front of me. She was about a foot high. She was wearing a dress made of two layers of flower petals. The outer layer was bright red, the inner layer soft pink. Her green cap looked like the base of a flower.

And she had wings!

It took me a minute to see that they were fake.

Even though she was dressed like a fairy, she had the ugliest little face I had ever seen. Her nose was about two sizes too big for her head. So were her pointy ears. And she had a pair of fangs that made me nervous.

"Put me down, ya big doot!" she said, squirming wildly.

"If I do, will you promise not to jump on me again?"

"Yeah, yeah, yeah. I promise."

The way she said it made me wonder what her promise was worth. But I put her down anyway—mostly because she was squirming so hard that I didn't think I could hold her much longer even if I wanted to.

"Come on," I said. "Moongobble is inside—"

My words were cut off by a loud boom.

Thick green smoke poured through the cottage window.

"Uh-oh," said Fireball. "What's Moongobble done now?"

CHAPTER 2

TINY CAT

With Fireball still clinging to my shoulder, I stepped into the cottage. The green smoke was so thick, I could barely see a foot ahead of me.

"Good grief," croaked a deep voice. "You've messed up *again*, Moongobble!"

I knew that voice. It was Urk the Toad.

"Well, at least it wasn't cheese!" said Moongobble cheerfully. He coughed, then added, "At least, I don't think it's cheese. I can't see yet."

"Neither can I," said Urk. "We have to get rid of this dad-ratted smoke."

I grabbed the door and swung it back and forth, creating a swirl of air. At the same time Fireball flew around the room, flapping like crazy.

The smoke began to drift out the door.

"Well, that's better," said Urk. "Wait a minute. *Wait a minute!* Good grief. Moongobble, look what you've done!"

"What?" asked Moongobble. "What is it?"

Wondering what magical mess Moongobble had made now, I waded through the remaining smoke, waving my hands in front of me. Finally I saw Moongobble. He was standing at one end of the big table.

He looked very unhappy.

As more smoke cleared, I spotted a tiny blue cat at the other end of the table. The cat couldn't have been more than six inches long. Even so, it was clearly a cat, not a kitten. It had lifted one paw and was staring at it in horror.

The mice who live in Moongobble's hat shrieked and pulled their door shut.

"Sissies!" snapped the cat.

I knew that voice! "Urk?" I asked in astonishment.

"Yes, I'm Urk!"

"Uh-oh," whispered Fireball.

"Oh, my," said Moongobble, sounding embarrassed. "Oh, I am so sorry, Urk. I'll turn you back as quick as I can."

"How? With another one of your spells?"

"Of course," said Moongobble. Raising his wand, he cried, "Iggledy! Biggledy! Fixxum Dacat!"

BOOM!

More smoke billowed around us.

When it cleared, I saw that Moongobble had indeed changed Urk.

Oh, he was still a cat.

But now he was bright pink.

"Gaaaaah!" cried the former toad. "Pink! I *hate* pink!"

Moongobble raised his wand again.

"Stop!" cried Urk. "Just stop right there!"

"Now calm down," said Moongobble.

"Calm down? I'm a cat. I hate cats. Not only am I a cat, I'm pink! A little pink cat! Do you have any idea how humiliating this is?"

"I think you're cute!" said a tiny voice.

That was when I realized the annoying new-comer had slipped into the cottage with us. Not only had she come into the cottage, she had climbed the table leg. Now she was standing between me and Moongobble.

"Who are *you*?" demanded Urk.

"My name is Snelly. Can I have you? You're just the right size for a pet."

"No, you cannot have me! And I am *not* a pet!"

"But I wanna hug you and kiss you and wrap you in a blanket!" cried Snelly, darting toward him.

I lunged forward. Grabbing her fake wings, I snatched her off the table.

"Let me go, ya big brute!" she bellowed, trying to wriggle out of my grasp. *"Let me go!"*

"Not until you promise not to touch the kitty."

"I am *not* a kitty!" roared Urk.

"Yes you are, and I love you!" cried Snelly.

"Moongobble!" bellowed Urk. "DO something!"

"I'm thinking!" said Moongobble. "I'm thinking!"

"That's what I was afraid of," muttered Urk.

"Let me go!" squealed Snelly, still squirming.

"Do you promise not to touch Urk?" I asked.

Snelly held still. "I promise."

I looked around the room. "If you break your promise, I'll put you in that birdcage."

"You're a booger! Besides, I already promised. Let me go!"

I set Snelly on the table but stayed ready to grab her if she darted toward Urk again.

She crossed her arms and glared at me.

Moongobble fetched one of his books of magic from the shelves.

"Maybe the spell will just wear off after a while," I whispered to Urk.

"Yeah, and maybe I'll learn to fart flowers."

As a tiny pink cat, Urk was cuter than he used to be. Unfortunately his personality was the same as ever.

Just then we heard a loud buzz. We knew that sound well. It meant Fazwad was about to arrive.

"Don't tell him who I am!" cried Urk in a panic.

Though the Head of the Society of Magicians was now our friend, he and Urk still did not get along.

With a loud snap and a burst of blue smoke, Fazwad appeared. "Greetings, Moongobble!" he cried. "I've come to talk to you about—"

He stopped. His eyes grew wide. Pointing at Snelly, he cried, "What in the name of Bald Bertha's Beard is *she* doing here?"

It was the first time I ever saw Fazwad look frightened.

CHAPTER 3

LITTLE MONSTER

"Here, now, Fazwad," said Moongobble. "That's no way to talk about a little girl."

"You don't know her, Moongobble! She's trouble wrapped in flower petals, disaster with a turned up nose. Her mother is Queen of the Mischief Monsters! We've got to get her home—and fast!"

"I don't wanna go home," said Snelly, crossing her arms and plunking down on the table.

"Ah, in trouble with your mother, are you?" asked Fazwad.

12

Snelly blushed, which I wouldn't have thought possible.

Fazwad looked at her more carefully. "How did you get here, anyway?" he asked, tapping his chin. "You're farther from home than you ought to be able to go on your own."

"I'm not telling!" said Snelly. She jumped up. "Come here, little cat. I wanna pet you!"

Fazwad turned to Moongobble. "You have a problem, my friend."

I still had trouble getting used to Fazwad calling Moongobble "friend."

"I don't understand," said Moongobble.

Fazwad sighed. "Sooner or later Snelly's mother will notice she's missing—probably when things start to seem too quiet. If she finds out Snelly is here and we've kept her, she'll start a Mischief

War." He shuddered. "You don't know the meaning of 'annoying' until you've been caught in a Mischief War."

"He's not kidding, Moongobble," said Urk.

Fazwad squinted at the little pink cat, then grinned. "I know that voice!"

He sounded more amused than I thought was polite.

"When will I learn to keep my big mouth shut?" groaned Urk.

Fazwad raised an eyebrow. "Another spell gone wrong, Moongobble? We really must get you to Flitwick City for some extra training. Ah well, cheer up, Urk. It could be worse. At least you're not cheese!"

"Thanks. I feel better already."

"I won't go home!" said Snelly, who had found the glue pot and was struggling to open it.

"Oh yes you will," said Fazwad. "And Moongobble is going to take you there."

"Hey," I said as I snatched the glue pot from Snelly. "Moongobble has already performed his three Mighty Tasks."

"Indeed he has, Edward. However this is not a

Mighty Task. It is an Official Assignment. They are different things."

"Say no, Moongobble," urged Urk.

Fazwad looked serious. "Moongobble wanted to join the Society of Magicians, Urk. He got his wish. Membership has privileges, but it also has responsibilities. Since Snelly came to Moongobble's home, it is his task to return her."

"Of course," said Moongobble. "I'll be glad to do it."

"Good." Holding out his right hand, Fazwad snapped his fingers. With a puff of blue smoke, a piece of paper appeared. "This map will show you the way."

He placed the map on the table.

Urk trotted over on his little pink feet to look at it. "Oh, no," he groaned.

CHAPTER 4

FAMILY CURSE

"What's the matter?" I asked.

"This kid lives in Monster Mountain!" said Urk.

"Monster Mountain?" asked Moongobble. "What's that?"

Urk shook his head. "Let's just say the place didn't get its name by accident."

"You are correct to say she lives *in* the mountain, Urk," said Fazwad. "Monster Hall, the home of the Mischief Monsters, is located in a cavern deep inside the mountain." Pointing at a spot on the map, he added, "You'll find the entrance here. Once you reach this place, the map will change to show the underground path."

"That's very clever!" said Moongobble.

"Yes, isn't it? Well, I must be going. Oh, I nearly forgot! I came to invite you to your first meeting of the Society of Magicians, Moongobble. It will be next Tuesday. You should be back by then . . . assuming all goes well."

With a snap of his fingers, Fazwad disappeared.

"I don't care that he's nice now," said Urk, waving away a trace of blue smoke. "I still don't like that guy."

"I like *you*," said Snelly. "You're the cutest little pink cat in the world!"

"I'm probably the *only* little pink cat in the world," snarled Urk. "Just don't forget—I've got little pink claws!"

Snelly stuck out her tongue at him. Then she sat on the table, smiled up at us, and said, "By the way, I'm not going home."

"Oh yes you are," said Moongobble. "You heard Fazwad."

"He's not the boss of me!"

"Well, he's the boss of me. Besides, you belong with your mother."

"But she's mean to me," said Snelly, beginning to cry. "She's terrible, terrible mean!"

Moongobble looked concerned. "How is she mean to you?"

"Last week she said I was naughty."

"And why did she say that?" asked Urk.

"Because I tied knots in her hair while she was asleep."

"Well, that *was* naughty, wasn't it?" I asked.

"Yes," said Snelly, pouting. "But she didn't have to *say* so. Besides, I'm a Mischief Monster. I'm *supposed* to be naughty!" She leaped to her feet. "Come here, little cat. I wanna hug you."

Urk jumped off the table. Snelly stamped her foot, then started after him. Moongobble grabbed her as she went by.

"Let me go, ya big meanie!" she cried, flailing her arms and legs. "Let me go!"

"Edward," said Moongobble. "Get the birdcage!"

"No, no, *no*, NO, *NO!*" shrieked Snelly, struggling harder than ever.

I fetched the birdcage. Moongobble thrust Snelly inside, then closed the door as quickly as he could. Turning to me, he said, "Hold the door shut while I use a spell to lock it."

I pinched the door tight to the bars of the cage.

"Let me out, ya big bully!" cried Snelly. "Let me out!" She grabbed my fingers and pulled at them.

Raising his wand, Moongobble cried, "Iggle, Biggle, Clozzem Dadoorski!"

A burst of green light nearly blinded me.

I blinked twice, then saw that the cage had turned into a big box with no windows.

"Let me outta here!" screamed Snelly. "I'm afraid of the dark!"

Moongobble sighed and tapped his wand against the table. It only took him three tries to get the cage back to its regular shape, one try after that to get a lock on it, and one more try after that to turn the clump of cheese at the end of my arm back into a hand.

"Should we invite the Rusty Knight to come along?" I asked after I had counted my fingers to make sure they were all there.

"He's come on all our other trips," said

Moongobble. "Probably he should come on this one, too."

So we headed for the Rusty Knight's cottage.

We made an unusual sight going through Pigbone: a boy, a magician, a four-foot dragon, a tiny pink cat, and a Mischief Monster locked in a birdcage that Moongobble carried on a stick over his shoulder.

Even so, no one came out to bother us.

That might have been because of the way Snelly was carrying on. "Help!" she screamed. "Help! Help! Robbers! Fire! Murder and bandits! Floods! *Earrrrrrrthquaaaaaake!*"

Fortunately Pigbone only has fifteen cottages, so it didn't take long to get to the Rusty Knight's. It's the nicest cottage of all, with a big garden and real glass windows.

To our surprise, our friend was not at home.

At first we thought he must have gone on an errand. Then we found this note on his door:

Dear Friends,
*   I have been called away on an important task.*

Well, if you must know, I have to deal with an old family curse. Please wish me luck.

I hope to return to Pigbone someday. If I do not, know that I have loved living here, and will miss you all.

Your friend,
The Rusty Knight

CHAPTER 5

THE ROAD TO MONSTER MOUNTAIN

"I don't like the sound of that," said Urk.

"Neither do I," said Moongobble. "I wonder why he didn't come to us for help."

I was wondering the same thing. The Rusty Knight always helped us when we asked, so it seemed as if it should have been our turn to help him.

"Maybe he was embarrassed," said Urk. "Old family curses can be pretty nasty."

"What a wise little pink cat," said Snelly, sticking her hands through the bars of the cage. "Come here so I can give you a kiss."

Urk stuck his tongue out at Snelly. Then he stuck it out again, and crossed his eyes trying to see it. "What a stupid excuse for a tongue," he muttered. "I'll never catch flies with this!"

Ignoring Urk, Moongobble said, "We will have to travel without the Rusty Knight. But as soon as we return, we will do all we can to track him down so we can help him. Now, come along. Let's get ready. Oh, dear. I hope your parents won't be too upset about this, Edward. I promised to keep you out of trouble."

"I'm sure it will be fine," I said. "They certainly wouldn't want you to leave me on my own. And you have to take Snelly home. So there's really no choice."

I tried not to sound too happy. But getting permission to go on a trip with Moongobble was always a bit of a fuss. So it was nice that for once I didn't have to worry about it!

"Mother used to tell me she was going to send me to Monster Mountain when I was naughty," I said to Urk as we entered the forest behind Moongobble's cottage that afternoon.

Urk looked startled. "But Monster Mountain is

a terrible place. All kinds of strange things happen there!"

"I don't think she really would have done it!" I said, feeling as if I had betrayed Mother by saying this. "It was just a way to get me to behave."

"Oh, well, parents," said Urk with a little pink shrug. "Who knows what goes on in *their* heads?"

"Monster Mountain isn't so bad," said Snelly, clutching the bars of her cage. "I like it there!"

"Then why did you run away?" asked Urk quickly.

"None of your beeswax! Come here, I wanna pet you!"

She began shaking the bars of the birdcage. Fortunately they didn't break.

"Come on, little cat!" whined Snelly. "I wanna pet you!"

"Walk faster, Moongobble," said Urk. "The sooner we get her home, the better."

After we had gone a little way, Moongobble put Urk on his shoulder so he could help read Fazwad's map. (Urk's main job was to make sure Moongobble didn't hold the map upside down.) At first Urk slipped and slid on Moongobble's robe, but finally he figured out how to hook his claws into the cloth. "Riding here was easier when I was a toad," he muttered crankily. "This darn pink fur is slippery!"

Fireball fluttered along above us, sometimes racing forward, sometimes shooting out little bits of fire. I wasn't sure, but I thought he was frying bugs.

It felt very strange to be traveling without the Rusty Knight. He had joined us for all our other journeys.

"Turn here," said Urk suddenly, pointing to a fork in the path.

We turned and entered a section of the forest that was so gloomy, it looked like it was twilight, even though I knew the sun was still high in the sky.

We had gone only a few hundred feet into the gloom when I spotted a glove on the ground.

I recognized it at once.

It belonged to the Rusty Knight.

CHAPTER 6

WE ENTER MONSTER MOUNTAIN

"What's this doing here?" asked Moongobble, picking up the glove.

"I suppose it means the Rusty Knight came this way," said Fireball, fluttering down for a closer look.

"That family curse must be pretty awful it if brought him *here*," muttered Urk, looking around at the gloomy forest.

Suddenly Snelly screamed, "Look out! Bandits!"

I spun around, bracing myself for danger.

"Made you look!" she shrieked, laughing so hard, snot bubbled out of her nose.

"You stop that, Snelly!" ordered Moongobble. "There's no telling who—or what—you might attract if you keep that up."

"Then let me out of this cage!"

"I can't do that. You'll run away!"

"I will not."

"She will too," said Urk.

"Not if you let me walk with the pink kitty I won't," said Snelly.

Urk groaned. "Don't believe her, Moongobble."

"Help! Help! Bandits! *Robbers!*"

"Can't you cast a spell of silence on her?" I asked Moongobble.

"I don't dare. What if something goes wrong? We can't risk starting a Mischief War."

"I know!" cried Urk. "Make her promise on her mother's nose hairs."

"What?" I asked.

"I just remembered. It's a sacred oath for little monsters like her. Even Snelly wouldn't dare break it."

"How do *you* know that?" asked Snelly. She sounded angry.

I was wondering the same thing. But all Urk said

was, "I know lots of things, missy. And if you want to get out of that cage, promise on your mother's nose hairs that you won't try to run away from us." He thought for a second, then added, "Also that you won't try to grab me!"

"Oh, all right," said Snelly, sounding vexed. "I promise!"

"On your mother's nose hairs?" asked Moongobble.

"On my mother's nose hairs," grumbled Snelly.

Moongobble opened the cage door.

"You guys are mean," said Snelly.

We started walking again. We hadn't had much of a rest, but it was better than listening to Snelly complain.

The path went uphill, becoming steeper and steeper.

After a while, Urk said darkly, "According to the map, we are now on Monster Mountain."

I felt a chill.

Toward the end of the day we reached a cave.

"This is it," said Urk. "The entrance to Monster Mountain."

Two big boulders sat just over the cave. They

looked like big eyes—which made the cave itself look like a giant mouth.

"How are we going to see once we're in there?" I asked.

"Don't worry," said Moongobble. "I'll fix up something."

"Then it's time to worry," said Urk.

Moongobble rolled up his sleeves to cast a spell. As he began to chant, I stepped away, for safety's sake. Urk, Fireball, and even Snelly came with me.

Waving his hands, Moongobble chanted, "Iggle, Biggle, Ternon Daglo!"

His hat fizzed, then began to glow. It was dim at first, but soon it looked as if he had a small moon on his head. The mice who live inside his hat shrieked, then scampered down his back and into one of his pockets.

"Well," said Urk, "I'm guessing that wasn't what you intended. But you did actually get something useful on the first try. It's progress."

Moongobble sighed. "I suppose this will have to do. Well, let's get moving."

With Moongobble in the lead, we stepped

inside Monster Mountain. The rocky walls of the tunnel, smooth and shiny, reflected the glow from Moongobble's hat. In the distance I could hear water dripping. Long fingers of slick stone reached down from the ceiling. They were solid and didn't move. Even so, I felt as if they were trying to catch me.

It was a long walk to Snelly's home, and we got

lost more than once. But we also saw many amazing things, like an underground lake. Only, the lake made me nervous, because I could hear things splashing around in it, and a couple of times I saw big eyes peering at us from just above the surface.

Snelly grew more nervous the closer we got to her home. "I don't want to go back!" she cried. "I don't want to go back! *Please* don't make me go back!"

I figured she must have done something really naughty.

At last we saw a sign that said:

MONSTER HALL,
ONE MILE.

"I don't wanna go home!" wailed Snelly.

On we walked.

Before long we saw another sign. It said:

MONSTER HALL,
ONE-HALF MILE.
ARE YOU SURE YOU
WANT TO DO THIS?

"*I don't wanna go home!*" wailed Snelly again.

On we walked.

The next sign said:

MONSTER HALL,
ONE-QUARTER MILE.
WHAT ARE YOU, NUTS?!

"*I really, really don't wanna go home!*"

It was only a little way to the last sign, which said:

TOO LATE NOW!
DON'T SAY WE DIDN'T WARN YOU!

Which was when ten big monsters jumped out and grabbed us.

CHAPTER 7

MONSTER HALL

The monsters looked a lot like Snelly. At least they looked the way Snelly might look if she was six feet tall, a boy, and covered with big muscles.

I think their tunics had been stitched together from dried mushrooms.

"Oh ho!" cried one of them. "It's the wicked little runaway! The queen will be glad to see her."

Snelly nudged me and hissed, "I told you I didn't want to go back!"

"I don't know why the queen would care," said

another monster. "She's an awful pain in the butt-a-rooni."

"Shut yer gob, ya big doot!" cried Snelly. Then she stuck out her tongue and made a very rude sound.

This seemed like a bad idea to me.

"You with the shiny hat," said the first monster, pointing to Moongobble. "Turn it down."

"Snotfork is right," said another monster. "You're hurting my eyes."

Moongobble muttered a spell. His hat kept glowing, but now it was green.

"That's better," said Snotfork. "All right, let's get going. Hup! Hup! Hup!"

With five monsters in front and five behind, we started walking again.

"How come they're so big and you're so small?" I whispered to Snelly.

"You can't start out that big when you come out of an egg," she said, as if I were really stupid. "It takes a while to grow, you know."

"You were *hatched*?" I asked in amazement.

Snelly sighed and rolled her eyes.

Soon we came to a big set of doors. The lead

monster, Snotfork, banged on them.

They swung open.

I gasped. On the other side of the doors was a cavern so high that I couldn't see the ceiling, and so wide that I couldn't see the far side. What I *could* see was Monster Hall, which turned out to be a huge stone castle inside the cavern. It had high towers, a wide moat, and a drawbridge you had to cross to get inside.

The reason I could see all this, even underground, was that about every five feet a stone arm stuck out from the castle walls. Hanging from each of these arms was a glowing basket.

I was wondering what made the baskets glow when Snotfork banged his stick against one that hung from the cavern wall and bellowed, "Turn on, you lazy things!"

"All right, all right," replied a small voice. "Sheesh. You don't have to be in such a hurry."

The basket began to shine. That was when I realized it was really a cage. Inside the cage were three lizards, each glowing as brightly as Moongobble's hat.

"That's better," grunted Snotfork.

"Oh, go eat a pickle," said the lizard who had spoken before. "We don't have to turn on until someone asks us to, and you know it, Snotfork. So calm down." Turning toward Moongobble, the lizard added, "Nice hat!"

"Thank you," said Moongobble. "I made it myself."

"Enough!" snapped Snotfork. "Let's get going."

As we walked away, Fireball fluttered off my shoulder. Turning, I watched him flap back and land on the cage. He began hissing to the lizards.

"What were you doing?" I whispered when he came back.

"I asked if they wanted me to let them out."

"Why did you do that?"

"Well, they're cousins, sort of."

"What did they say?"

"They told me they were fine. It's their job. In another few hours the next shift will come on, and they can go home to their families."

"Shut up back there!" bellowed Snotfork.

Crossing the drawbridge, we entered Monster Hall.

CHAPTER 8

THE LOST PRINCE

The inside of Monster Hall was lit by more baskets. Several of the glowing lizards shouted friendly greetings to the guards as we passed. Others seemed to have a grudge against Snelly, since when they spotted her they called things, like "Uh-oh, someone's gonna get it!" and "Ooooh, look who's in trouble now!"

"That's strange," I said to Urk, who was riding on my shoulder. "They have rugs hanging on the walls."

"You don't get out much, do you, Edward? Those aren't rugs. They're tapestries."

"What are tapestries?"

"Rugs that you hang on the wall."

That didn't make much sense to me. Even so, the tapestries were interesting, because they had pictures woven into them. The pictures all showed monsters making mischief of one sort or another: balancing pails of water over doors, jumping out to scare people, hiding important things.

We came to a pair of stone doors. Each door had a face carved on the front. One face was laughing, the other sobbing.

"I don't wanna go in there!" cried Snelly.

The guards ignored her.

The doors swung open.

In we went.

A lady monster sat on the throne at the far end of the room. She was about three times the size of Snelly—which made her about half the size of the guards. She had bulging eyes, sprouts of hair growing out of her ears, and very big fangs. Other than that, she looked a lot like her daughter.

A big spider sat on the queen's shoulder. Suddenly the queen grabbed the spider and threw it right at

me. I screamed as it landed on my chest. Jumping back, I tried wildly to brush it off.

It took me longer than it should have to realize that the spider was made of cloth and paper.

The queen laughed until tears ran out of her eyes. "Oh, I love that trick," she gasped. Looking at us more closely, she spotted Snelly, who had been hiding behind Moongobble. "Ah, my runaway daughter! I must thank you for her return, who-ever you are. We have grief enough here as it is."

"I am Moongobble the Magician," said Moongobble, making a surprisingly good bow. "And these are my companions, Fireball the Dragon, Urk the Toad, and Edward the . . . Humble."

"I don't see a toad," said the queen.

Moongobble blushed. "An unfortunate accident has turned Urk into a little pink cat for the time being."

"And I like him that way!" cried Snelly.

"You spoke of grief," said Moongobble, ignoring Snelly. "Why do you grieve, your majesty?"

The queen's lower lip began to tremble. "I grieve because the prince-to-be has been stolen from us!"

"I didn't want a little brother," muttered Snelly.

"Is there any way we can be of help?" asked Moongobble.

The queen grabbed her lower lip and pulled it over her forehead.

"That means she's thinking," said Snelly.

After a moment the queen let go of her lip. It snapped back to its normal size. "The prince-to-be was stolen by our great enemy, Oggledy Nork, the most horrible creature in all these mountains. If you can regain the prince-to-be, I shall be deeply in your debt. So much so that, if you would like, I will change that little pink cat back into a toad."

"Hey!" cried Snelly. "I like him the way he is!"

"Quiet, child!" roared the queen in a voice so loud, it made me jump. Several of the guards jumped too, which made me feel better.

After her voice stopped echoing around the walls, the queen said, "Oggledy Nork lives in a fortress on the far side of Monster Mountain. I have already sent one hero to rescue the prince-to-be. Alas, he has failed me. I suspect he met a terrible end." She smiled. "For your sake, I hope you can do better."

CHAPTER 9

FORTRESS NORK

The plan was for us to start the next morning. I couldn't figure out how you were supposed to tell morning from night while underground, but the monsters seemed to think they knew.

The queen gave us a cave to sleep in, and some blankets that were made of dried mushrooms stitched together. Snelly tried to stay with us, of course, but her mother grabbed her and tucked her under one arm. "Oh no, my dear," she said. "You'll be staying with me!"

"Save me!" wailed Snelly, holding her arms out to us. "*Save me!*"

"Oh, stop," snapped the queen, "or I'll give you something for them to save you from!"

Snelly was still yelling as her mother carried her away.

"I don't like this, Moongobble," said Urk, once we were alone. "We were lucky when we met Fireball."

"Thank you," said Fireball, stretching his neck and preening a bit.

Urk scowled. "I simply mean you weren't as big and bad as we expected. That's not going to happen twice. Whoever—or whatever—Oggledy Nork is, he's bound to be either big or bad. Probably both. We should go home. I'd rather stay a pink cat forever than have Edward and Moongobble get eaten."

"Edward will not get eaten, because he is not to get anywhere near Oggledy Nork," said Moongobble firmly. "This is *my* job, and I intend to do it."

I gasped. "You're not saying we can't come with you, are you?"

"You'd better not even be thinking it," added Urk.

Moongobble sighed. "We will go to Fortress

Nork together. But once we get there, I'm the only one who's going in."

Urk looked at me and rolled his eyes.

The next morning the queen gave us a basket of mushrooms and a map to Fortress Nork. The map was a lot like the one we got from Fazwad, except I think the monsters made their paper out of mushrooms.

After several hours of walking through caves and caverns lit only by the green glow of Moongobble's hat, we stopped for a snack. When I opened the basket of mushrooms, a little voice said, "Boy, that's a relief. I thought you guys were never gonna take a break!"

"Snelly!" groaned Urk. "What are *you* doing here?"

"I came because I love you!" she cried, leaping out of the basket and throwing her arms around his neck.

"Now you just let go of me!" bellowed Urk.

"You don't have to be so mean," sniffed Snelly.

"And you don't have to be so dang huggy!"

"Should we take her back?" I asked.

Moongobble pondered this, then said, "I think we need to keep going."

"Yay for Moongobble!" cried Snelly.

She and Urk were still arguing when our path sloped upward. Soon we came out of the mountain. It was evening, and the sun was setting. Even so, the sudden light made us blink.

"Look!" I said, pointing straight ahead.

"Uh-oh," said Fireball, who was perched on my shoulder.

"Oh, my," said Moongobble.

"That can only be one place," said Urk.

We had reached the home of Oggledy Nork.

Fortress Nork was a crude castle made from boulders. Purple and red smoke curled from its big, crooked chimney. A circle of mushrooms, all of them taller than me, ringed it like a fence.

Scattered among the mushrooms were bones and skulls.

"This isn't worth it, Moongobble," said Urk. "I would rather be a pink cat all my life than have any of you get hurt."

"What a heroic little cat-toad!" cried Snelly. "You are so noble, it makes me want to cry. Even though I hate the prince-to-be, I will go get him. Then maybe you will let me cuddle you after all!"

With that, she dashed away from us.

"Snelly!" shouted Moongobble. "Snelly, you get back here!"

He was too late. The little stinker was plenty fast, as I already knew, and she was gone before any of us could stop her.

"I'll catch her!" said Fireball. He launched

himself from my shoulder. But before he could reach Snelly, she had darted into Oggledy Nork's house.

"Now what do we do?" I asked.

"I'll have to go and get her," said Moongobble. He sighed. "I was hoping we would have time to make a plan before I had to face Oggledy Nork. Ah, well—"

He took off his hat (its glow was bound to attract attention), rolled up his sleeves, and trotted toward the door.

I looked at Urk and Fireball.

"What are we waiting for?" said Urk.

We started after Moongobble.

The door of Fortress Nork was a foot thick, and three times as tall as me. It was also a little bit open—otherwise Snelly would never have been able to get in.

I wondered why Oggledy Nork had left his door open. Was he too stupid to close it?

Too big to bother with it?

Or was it a way to lure in strangers?

It was dark inside, and it took my eyes a moment to adjust.

When they did, I almost wished they hadn't.

The furniture was *huge*. I figured whoever sat in it must be huge, too.

I looked around for Snelly but couldn't spot her. Instead I saw something that surprised me so much I squawked.

"Shhh!" hissed Urk.

"But look," I whispered, pointing to the back of the room. "*Look!*"

Urk gasped.

CHAPTER 10

THE SECRET OF OGGLEDY NORK

Strapped into a chair so big it made him look like a doll was the Rusty Knight!

I ran to the chair.

The Rusty Knight was asleep. At least I hoped he was only sleeping. . . .

"Wake up!" I whispered urgently. "Rusty Knight, wake up!"

He didn't wake up. This was no surprise. His hearing is not very good, and I was trying to be quiet.

Moongobble, Urk, and Fireball joined me at the chair.

"Wake up!" hissed Fireball. "Rusty Knight, wake up!"

He didn't stir.

"For Pete's sake, wake up!" bellowed Urk.

The Rusty Knight *still* didn't wake up. But a voice from behind us thundered, "Who dare enter home of Oggledy Nork?"

We spun around in time to see a manlike creature stride into the room.

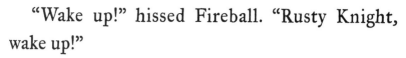

He was twice as tall as Moongobble, and dressed all in animal skins. His arms and legs were bare, which meant you could see his great, bulging muscles. Though his head was bald, clumps of hair sprouted from his shoulders and his elbows.

The smell that wafted from him made me want to throw up.

He carried a wooden club that looked as if it could flatten any one of us with a single blow.

Strangest of all, Snelly was clinging to his leg! She was so small compared to Oggledy Nork that at first I didn't notice her. When I did see her, I wondered if the little brat had betrayed us. So I was surprised when her first words were, "Why did you come in? I told you I would get the prince-to-be!"

"We came to protect you from Oggledy Nork," said Moongobble.

This made Oggledy Nork snort and growl. He lifted his club. I thought he was going to smash it down on Moongobble's head.

Moongobble raised his wand. At the same moment Fireball fluttered into the air, ready to spit fire.

Before either of them could do a thing, Snelly jumped down and ran to stand in front of us. "No, Oggledy Nork!" she cried. "No! Don't bash Moongobble. He's my friend!"

Oggledy Nork stared at Snelly in puzzlement.

"No smash little man?" he asked sadly.

"No," said Snelly firmly. "No smash little man!"

Suddenly Oggledy Nork looked hopeful. "Smash boy?"

Snelly shook her head.

"Teeny dragon?"

"No!"

Oggledy Nork smiled. He had at least four teeth. "Smash pretty pink kitty?"

"No, no, *no*, NO, *NO!*" screamed Snelly. She bounded over to snatch up Urk. "I *love* the pink kitty!"

For once Urk didn't try to squirm away from her.

"Then who *can* Oggledy Nork smash?" roared the towering creature, shaking his fist at the ceiling. "Oggledy Nork want to smash *someone!*"

His bellow was so loud it woke the Rusty Knight.

"Smash *me!*" he cried, struggling against the

bonds that held him in the chair. "Smash me! I deserve it!"

Oggledy Nork put down his club. A tear trickled out of his bulging yellow eye. "No," he said sadly. "Oggledy Nork no smash brother."

"*Brother?*" cried Moongobble, Urk, Fireball, and I, all at the same time.

The Rusty Knight sighed. "It's true. I am Oggledy Nork's brother. In fact I should *be* Oggledy Nork."

"Now that just doesn't make any sense," said Urk, who was still caught in Snelly's grip.

"No, it doesn't cost a single cent," agreed the Rusty Knight.

"Sense!" bellowed Urk, struggling to free himself from Snelly. "It doesn't make any *sense!*"

"It would if you knew the story," said the Rusty Knight.

"Well, I don't think we're going anywhere right now," snapped Urk. "And if you're his brother, why are you strapped in that chair?"

"Oggledy Nork strap brother in chair so brother not fall out while sleeping," said Oggledy Nork.

He pounded on his chest. "Oggledy Nork good brother!" Then he sat on the table, which groaned under his weight.

Snelly, who was still clutching Urk, trotted over to the ogre and said, "Wanna see my kitty-love?"

Oggledy Nork put down a giant hand. Urk's eyes widened as Snelly dropped him into the open palm.

"Don't run, kitty," said Snelly firmly. "That wouldn't be safe!"

Urk didn't run.

Oggledy Nork raised his hand to eye level. "What a nice pink kitty! Purr, kitty!"

Urk remained silent.

"PURR, KITTY!" roared Oggledy Nork.

Looking as if he had just swallowed a lemon, Urk began to purr.

"Does this have anything to do with that old family curse you talked about in the note you left on your door?" asked Moongobble, making sure to speak loudly enough for the Rusty Knight to hear.

The Rusty Knight nodded. "This is Fortress Nork, our family home. Long ago a curse was placed on the family. It said one son must always stay home and become Oggledy Nork. My brother and I had a contest to see who would stay, and who could enter the world. I won. But I have always felt bad that I left my brother here. So when I got a message that he was in trouble, I came to help him."

"Why was he in trouble?" asked Moongobble.

"Because of me," said Snelly softly.

CHAPTER 11

BROTHERLY LOVE

I looked at Snelly in amazement. "How could *you* get Oggledy Nork into trouble?"

She sniffed, then wiped her nose on her arm. "I brought the prince-to-be here and asked Oggy to keep him."

"Why did you do that?" I asked.

"Because I don't want a stinky little brother! Would you?"

"Sure. It would be fun."

"But I want my monster momma to love me best!"

I had to think about that. If I had a little brother, I would still want Mother to love me best. That wouldn't be fair, of course, but I would still want it. And it would be hard, because he would be cuter than me—babies are always cute—and need a lot of attention, too.

"I can see why you would be upset. But why would you give your little brother to a horrible monster like Oggledy Nork?"

"Oggy isn't horrible! He's sweet!"

"Me sweet," agreed Oggledy Nork, drooling and nodding happily. "Me like pretty pink kitty!" He looked down at Snelly. "What do kitties taste like, Snelly?"

"Bad!" bellowed Urk. "We taste really, really bad!"

Snelly looked alarmed. "Don't you dare eat him, Oggy! He's *my* pretty pink kitty!"

Oggledy Nork sighed. So did Urk. I could tell he was dying to bellow that he wasn't *anyone's* pretty pink kitty. To my relief, he managed to keep his mouth shut.

"What happened after you brought the prince-to-be here?" I asked Snelly.

"Nothing, for two or three days. Then Momma noticed he was missing."

I decided not to ask what kind of mother would need two or three days to notice her son was missing. Instead I just said, "Then what happened?"

"Momma got awful upset. Then she used her magic to find out where the prince-to-be was. I was sure lucky the magic couldn't tell her *I* was the one who brought him here! But it got poor Oggledy Nork in big trouble. That was when Momma sent a messenger to get the Rusty Knight. She wanted him to come talk to his brother, before we had to have a war with him. That was when I decided to run away. Only I didn't know where to go. So I just followed the messenger to Pigbone."

"I left as soon as I got the message, of course," put in the Rusty Knight. "And when the queen told me Oggledy Nork had stolen the prince-to-be, I headed straight for my old home. But I fell ill along the way. By the time I got here, I was so sick I couldn't even talk."

"Poor brother," said Oggledy Nork sadly, patting the Rusty Knight's head with one huge finger.

Snelly picked up her story. "I was still afraid to go home, so I stayed in Pigbone for a few days." She grinned. "I got into some pretty good mischief, too! Then I heard someone talking about the magician on the hill. That was when I came to your house, Moongobble. I thought you might be able to help me."

Moongobble smiled at this.

"Of course, that was before I found out you weren't very good at doing magic."

Moongobble's smile faded a little.

"Why didn't you just go get your brother yourself?" I asked.

"Because I was afraid that this time someone would follow me and Momma would find out what I had done! But I don't want Oggy to be in trouble either." She sniffed and wiped away a tear. "I didn't know what to do! I still don't!"

"Can I talk to your little brother?" I asked.

"Don't be stupid. He can't talk."

"Well, can I at least see him?"

Snelly sighed. "I suppose so. But just you! Come on, Oggy. We're going to take Edward to see Stinky-Pie. That's what I call him," she added, turning to me. "Stinky-Pie."

"Stinky-Pie," agreed Oggledy Nork happily.

Moongobble looked worried. Putting his hand on my shoulder, he said, "Edward, I can't let you go off alone with that monster."

"He'll be fine!" said the Rusty Knight firmly. "I promise on my honor as a knight!"

Moongobble paused, then nodded. "All right, go ahead. *But be careful!*"

I followed Snelly and Oggledy Nork out of the room. We climbed a rickety stairway, and then another. We came to a long hall. The floor tipped sideways. None of the walls were straight.

We stopped outside a door.

"Stinky-Pie's in there," said Snelly glumly.

Oggledy Nork pushed the door open. I stepped past him, then cried out in surprise.

"*That's* the prince-to-be?"

CHAPTER 12

THE PRINCE-TO-BE

Sitting in the center of the room was a box.

In the center of the box was a pillow.

Resting on the pillow was a big egg covered with orange and blue speckles.

Snelly walked over and stuck her tongue out at the egg. "Who asked for you, anyway, Stinky-Pie?"

I was relieved. I had tried to imagine Oggledy Nork taking care of a baby, but couldn't. But since the prince-to-be was only an egg, it must be all right. (Clearly, the queen had not spent all her time sitting on it!)

"Snelly," I said. "Do you love the pretty pink kitty?"

"More than anything in the world!"

"Do you want him to be happy?"

She looked at me suspiciously. "I want us *both* to be happy!"

"Do you love him enough to let him be himself?"

"You mean a toad? Sure. He's cuter as a kitty, but he'd be a pretty good toad, too."

"Then we have to take the prince-to-be back to your mother. If we do, she will turn Urk back into his real self, like she promised. He will not be happy if he has to stay a kitty."

"I know, I know," said Snelly with a sigh. Turning to the egg she muttered, "All right, Stinky-Pie, I guess we have to take you home."

I picked up the pillow. Carrying it very, *very* carefully, I followed Snelly and Oggledy Nork down the stairs.

Except for the two times that Snelly tried to convince us to leave the egg in the forest, and the three times that she tried to kiss Urk, our return to Monster Hall went smoothly.

When we got there, the queen greeted us with delight. "You've found the prince-to-be!" she cried, snatching up the pillow. "Oh, my precious, my precious, my precious!"

Then she kissed the egg five times.

"How do you know it's a prince, and not a princess?" asked Moongobble.

The queen crossed her eyes at him and said, "What a silly question!"

Then she kissed the egg again.

Snelly poked me in the leg. "See why I wanted to leave him with Oggledy Nork?"

That night the queen took us to a small cave. She lit a fire that burned bright green. The mice in Moongobble's hat peered out in fascination as she tossed in powders that made flashes of flame and puffs of colored smoke.

When everything was ready, she picked up Urk and chanted:

Farkledy, Arkledy, backward start,
Change to toad, part by part,
Hesperus, Zesperus, Bartleby Zort,
Shed that fur and grow that wart!
Piggledy, Higgledy, don't stop now!
Start to croak, good-bye meow.
Diddledy, Fiddledy, Stinky Pee-eeu,
Change your shape and just be you!

A loud bang echoed off the walls. A sudden puff of purple smoke surrounded Urk, hiding him from sight.

"Whoo-eee!" he said. "That stuff stinks!"

The queen cried, "Begone, smoke!"

The smoke vanished.

"I need to learn *that* trick," murmured Moongobble.

With the smoke gone I could see a familiar form sitting in the queen's hands.

"Hey!" cried Urk, lifting his front foot to examine his toadly toes. "I'm ME!"

"What did you expect?" asked the queen. "Did I not promise to turn you back?"

Moongobble made a deep bow. "Madame, I am most impressed."

"And I am most grateful," added Urk.

"You bad mommy!" cried Snelly. "I liked Urkie the way he was!" Then she plucked Urk from the queen's hands and hugged him. "But you are still cute, and I will love you forever and ever!"

"Help!" cried Urk, struggling to escape her grasp. "Someone save me!"

I wanted to pull him away, but I wasn't sure what the queen would do.

Urk managed to save himself. Wriggling free of Snelly's grasp, he dropped to the floor then hopped over to hide behind my leg.

"You bad toad!" cried Snelly. But before she could grab Urk again, a monster trotted into the cave.

He was carrying the pillow with the prince-to-be on it.

"Look!" he cried, pointing to the egg. *"Look!"*

CHAPTER 13

A NEW TASK

As we gathered around, I saw that the egg was shaking.

A crack appeared at the top of it.

A little hand pushed out. The hand began poking at the pieces of shell. Soon another hand reached up. The two hands tried to push the edges of the shell apart. Little grunts came from inside the egg.

"Should we help him?" whispered Moongobble.

"No!" said the queen sharply. "The prince-to-be must do this himself."

The shell quivered and wiggled—then split right down the middle.

Sitting in the center of it was an adorable baby monster.

"Goo!" he said.

It was the cutest sound I ever heard.

Snelly, who had been watching this with an angry frown, trotted over to the pillow. "You didn't tell me he would be so cute!" she said to her mother.

"He'll grow out of it!" said the queen, sounding slightly embarrassed.

"But I don't want

him to!" cried Snelly. "I want him to be cute forever!" She snatched the baby out of his eggshell. Holding him close, she crooned, "I am going to love you and cuddle you and teach you bad tricks!"

"What a good girl," murmured the queen, resting a hand on Snelly's head.

"Come on," whispered Urk. "Let's get out while the getting's good!"

I thought we would go home then.

I was wrong. We went back to Fortress Nork, where the Rusty Knight said, "I have been too selfish for too long. I must stay here and take care of my brother."

"How did this curse begin?" asked Moongobble.

The Rusty Knight tugged on his mustache. "Our great-great-great-great-something-or-other offended an old woman in the woods. She was so angry, she placed the curse of Oggledy Nork on him and his family, for all generations to come."

If there's one thing I've learned in the time I've been working for Moongobble, it's that you need to be careful of old ladies you meet in the woods.

"Is there any way to break the curse?" asked Urk.

"There must be," said Moongobble. "That's one of the rules of magic. There always has to be a counterspell."

"Well, why don't we go look for it?" asked Urk.

Moongobble rubbed his chin. "That's an excellent idea, Urk. The only thing is, we'll almost certainly have to take one of the brothers with us. But which one should we take?"

For a moment, no one spoke. Finally the Rusty Knight said, "I have been out in the world too long. My brother should go with you."

"If he goes, does that mean he'll turn back into himself and you'll turn into Oggledy Nork?" I asked.

The Rusty Knight shrugged. "The details of the curse weren't very clear."

Oggledy Nork patted him on the head. "What a nice brother," he said, drooling happily.

The next morning, Moongobble, Urk, Fireball, and I said farewell to the Rusty Knight. With Oggledy Nork tagging along behind, we headed for Pigbone, where we needed to pick up supplies—and tell my mother and father what we were going to do next. . . .

I wondered what they would say when they met Oggledy Nork.

Whatever they said, I knew one thing for absolute certain: If Moongobble was going on a quest for the way to break the curse of Oggledy Nork, I had to go along.

I just had to.